Snowy and the Rod of Power

Floella Benjamin

Illustrated by
FRANCIS MOSLEY

HEINEMANN:LONDON

To Aston

William Heinemann Ltd
10 Upper Grosvenor Street, London W1X 9PA

LONDON · MELBOURNE
JOHANNESBURG · AUCKLAND

First published 1987
Text © 1987 Floella Benjamin
Illustrations © 1987 Francis Mosley

A school pack of BANANA BOOKS 19–24 is
available from Heinemann Educational Books
ISBN 0 435 00103 5

ISBN 434 93045 8

Printed in Hong Kong by
Mandarin Offset

Chapter One

SNOTTY WILSON'S EYES shone
brightly in the darkness as he wiped his
sleeve absent-mindedly across his
running nose. It was this unfortunate
habit that had given rise to his
nickname.

Snotty was standing knee-deep in
water in a very dark and slimy cave. By

the light of his torch, he could see a long wooden box resting on a raised wooden platform. Carved on the side of the box in large letters were the words DO NOT OPEN. Snotty Wilson never took any notice of signs that began DO NOT and he wasn't about to start now. There had been a sign at the entrance to the cave saying DO NOT ENTER but he had entered it. There had been a sign at the far end of the beach where all the kids from The Sunny Rise Home for Unwanted Children had been taken by Mr and Mrs Scrogget. It said DO NOT GO BEYOND THIS POINT but Snotty had ignored that too. The fact that Mr and Mrs Scrogget and all the other kids were at this moment searching all over Limpsea for him didn't worry Snotty in the slightest.

He moved closer to the box and turned the rusty catch that kept it shut. The lid creaked as Snotty opened the box. There was a loud bang and bits of slimy stuff splattered down from the roof of the cave. Snotty jumped back, dropping his torch into the murky water and plunging himself into utter darkness.

'Oh, blow it!' cursed Snotty, fumbling under the water for the lost torch. It was then that he noticed the faint glow coming from the open box.

He stood up, wiped his sleeve across his nose again, and peered inside. There at the bottom, glowing weakly, was a long carved metal rod. Underneath was a small inscription. It read DO NOT TOUCH. Snotty reached into the box and picked up the rod.

5

It was about the size of a broomstick and very heavy. It glowed more brightly now and Snotty could see clearly enough to find his way back out of the cave onto the beach.

'Where the heck have you been, Wilson?' It was Mr Scrogget, his thin wisp of hair which was usually carefully arranged on the top of his head now blowing wildly about in the wind.

Mr Scrogget and his wife Hilda ran The Sunny Rise Home for Unwanted Children. Snotty hated him and if the truth be known Mr Scrogget didn't think much of Snotty either. Snotty wiped his sleeve across his nose and gave Mr Scrogget a dirty look.

'Right, get back to the mini-bus and stay there,' commanded Mr Scrogget.

Snotty felt the anger rising inside

him. Mr Scrogget was always having a go at him and he hated him for it.

'Push off, Scrogget,' replied Snotty. There was a bolt of blue light from the metal rod that Snotty was clutching and Mr Scrogget disappeared.

Snotty looked down at the rod which still had a wisp of blue smoke curling around its end. 'Oh brilliant,' he grinned. He looked closer at the rod and noticed that it had written down one side the words DO NOT USE in capital letters.

Chapter Two

VINCE AND LORNA had been
searching along the top of the cliffs for
Snotty when they had come across the
little cottage.

'Maybe Snotty's in there,' said Lorna.

Vince knocked on the door and after
a few seconds it was answered by an
old man. He was wearing a black

9

dressing-gown with moons and stars all
over it and he looked as if he hadn't
shaved for two or three months. Before
they could say anything, the old man
raised his hand.

'Quick!' he said. 'It's started.'

'Excuse me, but what's started?'
asked Lorna.

'The power has been used. Now we may not be able to stop it!' said the old man, pacing backwards and forwards and wringing his hands together.

'Let's run,' whispered Vince.

'No, don't go!' shouted the man. 'You've got to help me find it.'

'Find what?' said Lorna.

'You don't understand. Someone has got hold of the Rod of Power and they could destroy the entire universe!'

'Oh, is that all,' said Vince, trying to hold back the scream of panic that was welling inside his chest. 'Look out, he's a lunatic,' he hissed to Lorna who was staring at the man with her mouth hanging open.

'Er, where was this-er-Rod of Power?' asked Vince, trying to sound casual.

'In a cave down below,' said the old man, pacing backwards and forwards. 'You see, I'm the Guardian of The Rod and it's my job to stop anyone taking it.'

'If you don't mind me asking,' said Lorna 'How come you didn't stop whoever it was who took it, taking it?'

'I was having a kip.'

'Having a kip!' exclaimed Vince. 'That's a funny way to keep watch on it!'

'It's been all right up until now,' said the old man. 'I put a sign on the beach saying DO NOT GO BEYOND THIS POINT three hundred years ago and no one has ever gone past it.'

'Three hundred years!' Vince and Lorna both shouted at the same time.

'All right, so I'm new to the job but I'm doing my best.'

'Look,' stammered Vince, 'this is all getting a bit much. I think you'd better explain.'

'No time for that. You'll just have to trust me. Look, my name's Reg and I'm a wizard. The Rod of Power has been nicked and we've got to get it back or the entire universe could be destroyed . . . OK?'

Vince and Lorna stared first at each other, then at the strange old man who claimed he was a wizard called Reg. Then Vince broke the silence and spoke for them both.

'OK,' he said. 'We'll go along with you for the time being.'

'Wait a minute,' said Lorna, 'who do we know who always ignores signs that say DO NOT?'

'Snotty Wilson!' exclaimed Vince.

Chapter Three

THE WEATHER HAD turned nasty and
huge grey storm clouds were gathering
over the sea. Snotty was standing on
top of Parrot Hill which overlooked the
little seaside town of Limpsea. His
appearance had changed since his
encounter with Mr Scrogget.

A moment ago he had tested his new
found power by blasting the bandstand
on top of Parrot Hill into oblivion.
Fortunately the band weren't on it at
the time.

Snotty's face had a strange look of
mad power on it. His hair seemed to

have grown and it lashed around his
face in the howling wind. He had
ripped one of the real sheepskin seat
covers from Mr Scrogget's mini-bus
and wrapped it around him like a cloak.
He made a terrifying sight as he made
his way down the hill towards Limpsea.

Meanwhile, Mrs Scrogget had managed to get the rest of the kids back into the mini-bus and was heading into Limpsea to report the loss of Mr Scrogget, Vince, Lorna and Snotty Wilson to the police.

'We'll have to get the coastguard out,' she cried to the policeman on duty behind the desk. 'They've just disappeared, the lot of them.'

'That's not all that's disappeared,' said the policeman.

'What do you mean?' asked Mrs Scrogget, blowing her nose on a tissue.

'We've had reports coming in all afternoon of things disappearing. If you ask me, there's something funny going on.'

'Funny! . . . Flippin' incredible is what I call it, Constable.' The voice was that of Inspector Sergeant who had just

arrived at the police station. 'Don't worry, madam, we'll find your missing husband and the children. Right, Constable, has anything else gone missing since you called me on the phone?'

'Well, sir, apart from this lady's husband, the children and the bandstand, there's the fire station, a bus and the pier, sir.'

'Aha! Luckily the thief can't have got far. A pier is a pretty bulky item to conceal about one's person,' said Inspector Sergeant, rubbing his chin. 'We'd better get after them. Constable, bring your truncheon and a pair of handcuffs.'

Chapter Four

VINCE, LORNA and Wizard Reg had just made it to the top of Parrot Hill and were gazing down on the scene of destruction below.

'It's worse than I thought,' said Reg. 'It's taking him over.'

'What is this Rod of Power, anyway?' asked Vince.

'The rod once belonged to Gorag, the Mad Overlord of Thungor. It's charged with incredible power and anyone who holds it becomes incredibly nasty.'

'Well, Snotty Wilson was none too pleasant before he got hold of the rod, now he must be plain revolting!' said Vince. 'But why was the rod in Limpsea and why were you guarding it?'

'All the wizards got together one day and managed to get the rod away from Gorag. Then we hid it in a cave under the cliffs at Limpsea. One of us has always kept watch over it since then,' answered Reg.

'But why Limpsea?' asked Lorna.

Reg looked at Lorna and smiled. 'If you were Gorag, Mad Overlord of

Thungor, and someone took your Rod
of Power away, where's the last place in
the universe you would look for it?'

'Limpsea,' answered Lorna.

'Precisely!' said Reg, 'Now, come on,
we've got work to do. If young Snotty
keeps using the power, Gorag will be
able to home in on it and regain the
Rod.'

'And that will mean the end of the
universe?' said Lorna, who was
beginning to catch on.

'No,' said Reg, 'it's Snotty who could destroy the universe because he can't control the power of the rod. He could literally make the universe disappear.'

'So what happens if Gorag gets the rod back?' asked Lorna.

'There's no telling *what* he'd do,' said Reg, nervously tugging on his beard.

'You just wait till I get my hands on Snotty,' said Vince, 'I'll bash his head in.'

Snotty was striding up and down the deserted high street of Limpsea looking for a new target. He had his eye on the Town Hall and was about to take aim when a police car containing Inspector Sergeant and the Constable screeched round the corner, closely followed by Mrs Scrogget in the mini-bus.

'There he is!' shouted the Inspector. 'Head him off at the Amusement Park.'

Snotty fired a blast at the police car but it swerved just in time and the bolt of raw power hit the ladies' lavatory which disappeared in a cloud of steam. Snotty dodged through the gates of the Funland Amusement Park just as Reg, Vince and Lorna came rushing down the High Street.

'Leave this to me,' said Reg.

'No, we're coming with you,' said Lorna firmly.

'All right, but keep your heads down,' hissed the wizard.

Snotty ran to the big wheel and started it up. As the wheel slowly began to turn, Snotty leant back in the chair. From his vantage point he could see the whole town and he felt like the most powerful person on earth. He wiped his sleeve across his nose and read the sign in front of him: DO NOT LEAN OUT OF YOUR SEAT.

'Come down, Snotty, we've got you surrounded!' came the voice of Inspector Sergeant, who was standing next to the police car holding a megaphone. Snotty released another bolt of power from the rod and disintegrated the ground around the

car, leaving it and the Inspector
stranded on a little island.

'Right, that does it,' bellowed the
Inspector. 'Constable, arrest him.'

'But Inspector . . .   '

'That is an order.'

Chapter Five

S UDDENLY THERE WAS a clap of
thunder from the black storm clouds
above the park, followed by a flash of
lightning, and there stood Gorag, Mad
Overlord of Thungor.

He was nearly as tall as the big wheel and his face was level with Snotty's. His four eyes blazed with fire and his gigantic teeth dripped with green slime.

'Snotty,' came a voice that shook the whole of Limpsea, 'hand over my Rod of Power.'

Snotty snarled. He leant out of the chair and shouted, 'You're just like Mr Scrogget, you are. It's mine, so push off.'

Now being a Mad Overlord, Gorag wasn't used to people telling him to push off. He was more used to people grovelling to him and obeying his every command. But he had never had to deal with Snotty Wilson before. Mr Scrogget could have given Gorag a tip or two on how to deal with Snotty but he, of course, wasn't around. He was in

another dimension somewhere.

'I said push off!' screamed Snotty, pointing the rod at Gorag.

Gorag reeled back in disbelief as the bolt hit him in the chest.
There was a huge explosion and Gorag disappeared. The blast, however, threw Snotty from the chair and he plunged headlong towards the concrete below. Everyone watched in horror as Snotty plummeted down. Vince and Lorna noticed Reg put his hand out and mutter a magic word. For an instant,

Snotty seemed to hang in mid-air, then he began to float gently downwards like a feather and landed softly on the ground. During the fall, he had lost his hold on the rod and it had landed at Reg's feet. The wizard picked it up as Inspector Sergeant, the Constable, Mrs Scrogget and the children came running towards him.

'In all my years in the force,' began
Inspector Sergeant, 'I've . . .' But
before he could finish, Reg lifted his
hand and waved it in front of the two
policemen's faces. Their eyes glazed
over and Reg spoke in a commanding
voice. 'You will both forget everything
that has happened this afternoon,' he
said.

The Inspector and the Constable
walked back towards the police station,
their hands out in front of them.

Next Reg waved the Rod of Power and Mr Scrogget appeared, looking very angry.

'Snotty Wilson,' he spluttered, 'how dare you send me to another dimension! . . . It was very unpleasant there. . . . You wait till I get my hands on you. . . .' He started to lunge at Snotty but before he could reach him, Reg waved his hand and in a trice Mr Scrogget, along with Mrs Scrogget, Snotty and all the people of Limpsea, forgot everything that had happened that afternoon. Reg then replaced all the things that Snotty had blasted away, checked that the bandstand and the pier were back in position, and generally tidied up.

When he had finished he turned to Snotty, Vince and Lorna.

'I trust that you three can keep all this a secret,' said Reg.

'I don't think anyone would believe us if we told them,' said Lorna.

'True, very true,' laughed Reg. 'By the way, where is The Sunny Rise Home for Unwanted Children?'

'Oh,' said Vince, 'it's this old house

miles from anywhere; no one ever goes there.'

'Really,' said Reg, looking down at the Rod of Power, 'miles from anywhere you say.'

'Yes,' said Lorna, 'it's the last place on earth anyone. . . .'

Reg grinned and winked at Vince and Lorna. 'Be seeing you,' he said as he slowly disappeared into thin air.

Vince and Lorna turned and walked back towards the waiting mini-bus.

'You don't think he would. . . .' said Lorna.

Vince just shrugged. 'Well, Sunny Rise is the last place that Gorag would look, I suppose.'

'All right you lot,' came the voice of Mr Scrogget. 'Which one of you tore the real sheepskin cover off my seat? Snotty. . . !'